DINOSAURS AND DRAGONS

I wish, I wish
With all my heart
To fly with dragons
In a land apart.

By Margaret Snyder

Illustrated by The Thompson Brothers

Based on the characters by Ron Rodecker

Visit Dragon Tales on the Web at www.dragontales.com

Watch us on PBS!

One day, Max arrived in Dragon Land waving his favorite book high over his head. "Look what I've got!" he shouted when he spotted his good friend Ord.

Ord was searching for his ball, which had rolled away, but the big dragon stopped what he was doing and bounded over to greet Max.

"Hello, Max! What did you bring?" Ord asked excitedly.

"My dinosaur book!" Max replied. He opened the book and showed Ord a picture of a huge dinosaur. "This is an *Ultrasaurus*," Max said proudly. "It was one of the most gigantic dinosaurs that ever lived!"

"Wow!" said Ord. "It looks even bigger than my mom!"

Max showed Ord more of his book. "I love dinosaurs,"
Max said. "I wish I could find one, but they aren't around
anymore back home."

"I just wish I could find my ball," said Ord.

"I can help you do that," Max said, giggling. Together,
they began to look through the tall grass for Ord's lost ball.

"I found it!" Max shouted.
He pushed back the grass to reveal
something yellow and red and round.

Ord came running over. "That's not it. This is," he said, holding up his blue ball. "It was hidden under a mushroom."

Ord bent down to examine the yellow and red object more closely. "Max, you found an egg."

"An egg!" shouted Max excitedly. "Could it be a dinosaur egg?"

"I don't know," said Ord, puzzled. "It looks like a dragon egg to me."

Suddenly, lines appeared on the egg's shell. Then the egg cracked open and a small creature appeared.

"It's a dinosaur!" Max gasped.

"Really? How can you tell?" Ord asked.

Max opened his dinosaur book and showed Ord a picture. "Well, just look at the baby's back," Max said, pointing. "He has round bumps on his back just like this *Stegosaurus*!"

Then Max eyed Ord's back. "Gosh!" said Max with a giggle. "I guess you kind of look like a *Stegosaurus,* too."

Just then, the baby scurried over to a nearby bush and hungrily began chomping on dragonberries. "Look at him go!" Ord said.

"See! He *is* a dinosaur!" shouted Max. He held up his book and showed Ord a picture of another large dinosaur. "I bet he's a *Diplodocus*," said Max. "They were so big they had to eat all day long to get enough food."

"*Diplodocus* sounds like my kind of dinosaur," Ord said, smiling. He reached into his pouch and pulled out a huge sandwich. "Want some?" he asked.

Max shook his head and laughed as Ord gulped down the snack. "I guess some dragons can eat all day long, too," Max said.

Max flipped through his dinosaur book. "I'm sure I'll find a picture that looks just like the baby," he said.

"I think I have one," said Ord helpfully. He rummaged through his pouch and pulled out his own baby picture. Max stared at it. It did look a lot like the hatchling. Maybe Ord was right and it *was* a dragon after all.

Max scratched his head. "I wish there was a test for dinosaurs and dragons," he said.

That gave Ord an idea. "If he's a dragon, shouldn't he be able to breathe fire?" he asked.

Max agreed. He got down on his hands and knees and blew a puff of air at the baby. The baby puckered up his mouth as if he was going to blow right back. Max jumped out of the way, and out of the baby's mouth came an enormous burp.

"Now that I think of it, it took me a while before I could breathe fire, too," Ord said.

"How will we ever know if the baby is a dinosaur or a dragon?" Max asked with a sigh. Then he brightened. "We'll just have to look for more clues, that's all."

No sooner had Max spoken than he heard
a thundering sound.

"What was that?" Max gasped as the
ground shook.

"I think it's a clue!" said Ord.

The minute the baby saw the huge dragon, he jumped up and ran to her. "Ma-ma! Ma-ma!" the baby squealed.

Max and Ord looked on as the mother dragon scooped up her baby and gave him a big hug.

"Looks like he's a dragon for sure," Ord said.

"Wings!" Max said triumphantly as he spotted the small wings on the baby's back. "That's how you can tell a dragon from a dinosaur."

The mother dragon explained to Ord and Max how her egg
had rolled away from the nest. She had been searching for it all
day. She thanked them for finding her baby and taking such
good care of him.

"What's his name?" Max asked, patting the baby's head.

"I've had a hard time deciding," the mother dragon said.
"Do you have any ideas?"

Max looked at his dinosaur book and spotted the *Tyrannosaurus rex*. "How about Rex?" he suggested.

"I like it!" the mother dragon declared. "Rex it is."

Max giggled as Rex grabbed his finger. "So he is a little bit of a dinosaur after all."